THE LAST TOY

by T.E.Watson

Illustrated by Samantha LeDuc

Archway Publishing books may be ordered through booksellers or by contacting:

Archway Publishing
1663 Liberty Drive
Bloomington, IN 47403
www.archwaypublishing.com
844-669-3957

Because of the dynamic nature of the Internet, any web addresses or links contained in this book may have changed since publication and may no longer be valid. The views expressed in this work are solely those of the author and do not necessarily reflect the views of the publisher, and the publisher hereby disclaims any responsibility for them.

Any people depicted in stock imagery provided by Getty Images are models, and such images are being used for illustrative purposes only.
Certain stock imagery © Getty Images.

Interior Image Credit: Samantha LeDuc

ISBN: 978-1-6657-6619-7 (sc)
ISBN: 978-1-6657-6618-0 (hc)
ISBN: 978-1-6657-6617-3 (e)

Library of Congress Control Number: 2024919823

Print information available on the last page.

Archway Publishing rev. date: 10/09/2024

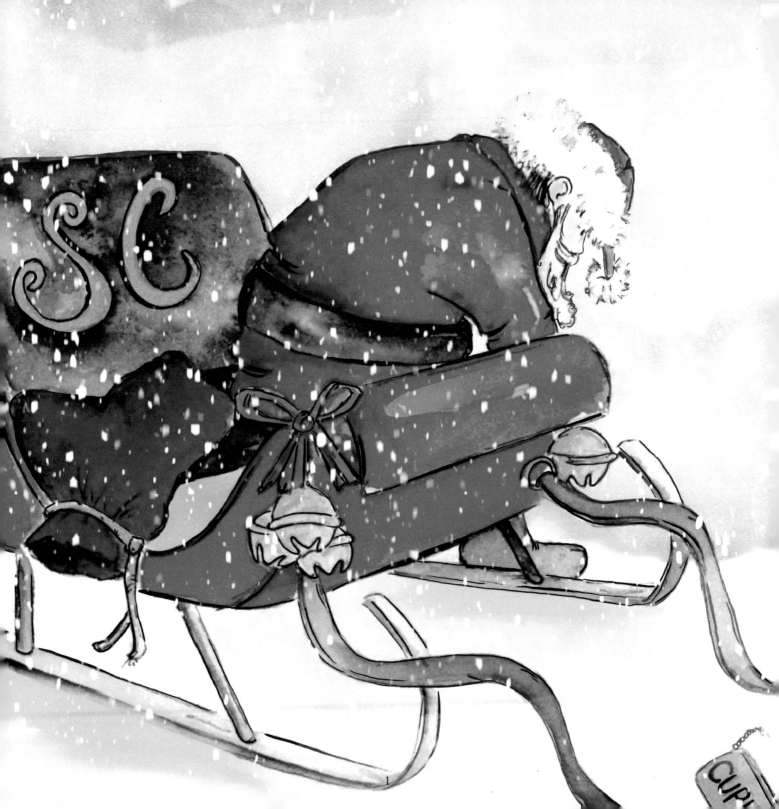

It was the day after Christmas, Santa ended his day.
His bag was all empty and so was his sleigh.

He climbed right on down and he picked up his sack,
when he heard the strange noise of a clickity clack.

What is that? Santa wondered, as he looked deep inside.
Oh, my word! He discovered, a toy tried to hide.

"But why little one? Now you're left all alone.
I delivered the others to safe and good homes."

"To all of the children, good girls and good boys.
I made sure that each one got their own special toys."

"So, tell me my friend, please tell me just why a home just for you has somehow slipped by."

"Let me see, my dear Santa, I will try to unfold
a marvelous story that's yet to be told."

14

"There was, once in a while, a time now and then.
A time that is happy, a time for all men."

16

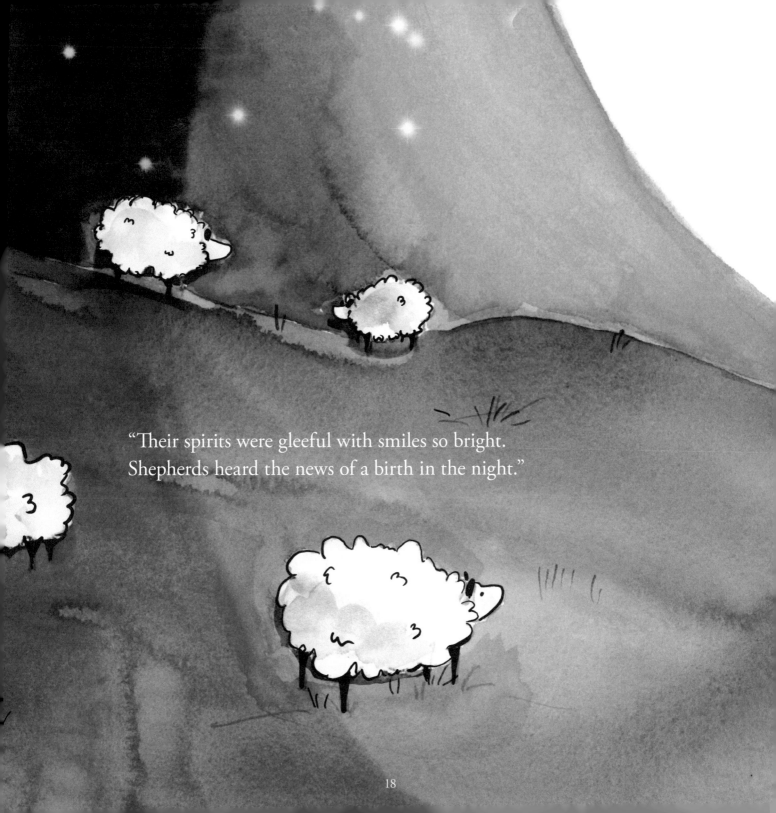

"Their spirits were gleeful with smiles so bright.
Shepherds heard the news of a birth in the night."

"A small special child of poverty born.
It is told he will live in scoff and in scorn."

19

"Now you know dear friend Santa why I hid deep away.
I am saving myself for a special birthday."

"Yes, I see little one. Your mission is clear.
We'll give you to him when the young one gets here."

25

With a touch of his nose and a twinkle of eye
They took off in a blink
into the night sky

With a Ho Ho Ho laugh, Santa soon spied a star.
"It's time we went out again. It doesn't look far."

"A special delivery you're about to complete.
We'll be guided by angels. Hold onto your seat."

Soon Santa delivered
the last special toy
And placed it right next to
The sweet little boy

31

I thank you dear Santa
For bringing me here
I wish you good tidings
And skies that are clear

Santa waved a goodbye
To the last little toy
And witnessed the smile
On that wee little boy

35

His wee face showed brightly
with a wonderful glow.
To remind us that Christmas is
the kindness we show

T. E. Watson
Author

It has been said that Award-Winning Children's **T. E. Watson** is the quintessential children's writer. Having written over 152 children's books, including 4 audiobooks for children. With every new story he generates, he continues to raise the standard for children's books.

His wonderful and never-resting imagination is always on the lookout for the friendly frog, wee Scottish Highland Faeries, or journey of friends trying to find a home.

His ability to bring us into the worlds in each of his stories makes him one of the brightest and foremost creative talents in children's literature.

He has studied extensively authors such as Sir J.M Barrie (Peter Pan), Mark Twain, Robert Louis Stevenson, and Roald Dahl. His research has won him major acclaim. His findings have helped him develop and write stories everyone enjoys.

Please see his stories such as The Man Who Spoke With Cats (winner of the Best Children's Book Award for 2009 by The America Authors Association, which also named him Best Author for the same year), Glen Robbie, a Scottish Fairy Tale, and A Place To Be (a story of loyalty and friendship).

The ever-favorite Mom Can I Have a Dragon and The Monster in the Mailbox. Just to name a few.

 He continues to surprise his readers with each new direction he takes. T.E. Watson can be contacted for school visits, speaking engagements, and conferences by emailing him at tew@tewatsononline.com.

Check out his website at www.tewatsononline.com

Illustrator: Samantha LeDuc

Samantha LeDuc is a watercolor artist who lives and works in Southern California. A native of Newmarket, England, her illustrations feature a unique blend of whimsy and realism, creating magical worlds where animals become storytellers, and children embark on extraordinary adventures. Her artwork possesses a gentle quality that resonates with both young and old, evoking a sense of nostalgia and longing for childhood innocence. For further information about Samantha and how she may be contacted go to www.samanthaleducillustrator.com

Printed in the United States
by Baker & Taylor Publisher Services